I0782230

Curtis

is a big brother now

ISBN 978-1-956001-47-1 (hardcover)
ISBN 978-1-956001-48-8 (eBook)

Printed in the United States of America

Curtis
is a big
brother
now
Doreen Barnett

I am going to the doctor's office with my mom.

I will be a big brother soon.

I get to teach him or her everything.

Now I have someone to play with. I'm so excited!

I can't go in the room with my mommy right now.
So, a nurse is watching me until mom
comes out of the room.

It's me and my mommy holding hands
walking out of the doctor's room.

Now that I'm going to be a big brother.
I have to clean up my room now.

Now, I have to help mommy do the dishes,

sweep the floor,

and take out the garbage.

Dad came home early today.
Mom is not feeling so good. Dad is taking mom
to the hospital. I hope everything is okay.

I have to stay with grandma for a couple
of days. I may be a big brother,
but I can't stay at home by myself.
Grandmas are the best because you can get
anything you want. You get hugs. You get kisses.
You get spoiled. You get anything.

My mommy and daddy are home.
I'm so excited! My mom's stomach is gone
and she doesn't look sick anymore.
Wait, wait! Mom has something in her
arms. Yay! I'm a big brother now.

Wow! We are a family. I'm happy but sad too.

Will Dad and Mom still love me?

Will I get hugs and kisses like before?

Will I be put to the side and be forgotten?

Dad and Mom noticed me starting to cry.
When Dad and Mom asked what was wrong,
I told them, "You might not love me anymore."

Mom says, "We will hug you, kiss you,
and love you all the time.
You don't have to worry about anything,
Dad and I will treat you just the same."

I am your big brother. My name is Curtis.
I will take care of you. I will teach you.
I will show you things because I am your big brother.

Everyone this is my little brother, Karl.